Sophie
and the
Seagull

Please visit our web site at: www.garethstevens.com
For a free color catalog describing Gareth Stevens Publishing's list of high-quality books
and multimedia programs, call 1-800-542-2595 (USA) or 1-800-387-3178 (Canada).
Gareth Stevens Publishing's fax: (414) 332-3567.

Library of Congress Cataloging-in-Publication Data

Fietzek, Petra, 1955-
    [Sofie und die Lachmöwe. English]
    Sophie and the seagull / written by Petra Fietzek; illustrated by Julia Ginsbach.—
North American ed.
       p. cm.
    Summary: Sophie likes to stay by herself, looking at everything through her telescope, until
she and the other children meet a one-legged seagull.
    ISBN 0-8368-3174-8 (lib. bdg.)
    1. Seagulls—Fiction. 2. Telescopes—Fiction. 3. Beaches—Fiction. 4. Friendship—Fiction.
I. Ginsbach, Julia, 1967-, ill. II. Title.
PZ7.F4792So   2002
[E]—dc21   2002017722

This North American edition first published in 2002 by
Gareth Stevens Publishing
A World Almanac Education Group Company
330 West Olive Street, Suite 100
Milwaukee, WI 53212 USA

Gareth Stevens editor: Dorothy L. Gibbs
Cover design: Tammy Gruenewald

This edition © 2002 by Gareth Stevens, Inc. First published as *Sofie und die Lachmöwe* © 2000
by Atlantis Kinderbücher, Verlag Pro Juventute, Zürich.

Printed in the United States of America

1 2 3 4 5 6 7 8 9 06 05 04 03 02

Sophie
and the
Seagull

Written by Petra Fietzek
Illustrated by Julia Ginsbach

Gareth Stevens Publishing
A WORLD ALMANAC EDUCATION GROUP COMPANY

Sophie stood at the window, looking at the sea through her telescope. She saw the waves, the lighthouse, and the boats. Somewhere out there, her father was on his fishing boat. Sophie's brother and sister were fighting over their toys. Sophie was glad to have her telescope.

Sophie's telescope is old, but she takes it wherever she goes, even to school.

"Why don't you play with the other children?" her teacher keeps asking her.

Sophie would rather watch the world through her telescope.

One windy day, while Sophie was watching the clouds, she heard children laughing. They were playing on a tree nearby.

"Sophie! Come here!" hollered a boy named Ollie.

Sophie pretended not to hear.

"Come on, Sophie!" all the children shouted, and they waved their arms at her.

"Something is moving in the bushes over there," called Ollie, pointing off into the distance. "Can you see anything through your telescope?"

Sophie couldn't help being curious. "What can it be?" she wondered, as she walked slowly toward the other children.

Sophie scrambled up the tree and looked through her telescope. There, behind the sand dunes, a bush was shaking as if a ghost were in it.

Sophie adjusted her telescope so she could
see the bush more clearly. A seagull was caught
in the brambles and was struggling to get free.

Sophie scurried down the tree and ran toward the bush. The other children followed her. When they reached the bush, the seagull was lying still, worn out from struggling. It was very weak and was stuck in the thorns.

Sophie picked up a stick that was lying in the sand and used it to carefully bend back the branches so the seagull could come out. But the bird didn't come out.

The children stood in the cold wind and waited. Suddenly, the seagull moved. It crept slowly out of the bush, then fell onto a patch of grass.

"Look!" Pete cried, "The seagull has only one leg."

"We should take it with us," Ollie declared.

But Sophie and the other children disagreed.

"We shouldn't touch it!" said Sophie.

"It might be sick!" said Pete.

Just then, the seagull ruffled its feathers, hopped a few times on its only leg, carefully tried its wings, and flew off.

"Goodbye, seagull," Ollie shouted after it.

At home that night, Sophie sat on her bedroom carpet, pretending she was on a big boat. She had climbed up its swaying mast to watch a jumping fish through her telescope.

Outside her bedroom window, the wind was rattling the shutters, and the sea thundered in the distance. There was another sound, too — a "tap-tap-tap" at the window.

When she heard the tapping, Sophie turned to see a shadow hopping up and down on the window sill. It was the one-legged seagull! Sophie raced to open the window.

"Wait!" she squealed with excitement. "Wait!"

She ran to the kitchen and grabbed some stale bread, then ran as fast as she could back to her bedroom. Sophie tossed pieces of the bread, one after another, out the window. The seagull snatched the bits of bread with its beak and gobbled them up. Then it shook its wings and flew off into the darkness.

After that night, the one-legged seagull visited Sophie every day, and Sophie waited eagerly. When she called to the bird quietly, it would hop close to her and stare at her with its tiny black eyes. Sometimes, they would play hide-and-seek outside the shed or around the trash cans.

"What fun!" thought Sophie, laughing with delight.

A few days later, the other children came to see Sophie and the seagull.

"I want to play!" said Ollie.

"We do, too!" shouted Pete and Hannah.

So, together, they all played hide-and-seek. The seagull could hop very well on its one leg, and it moved very fast. When it got tired, it just leaned against the shed.

Soon, other
seagulls joined
in the games.

The children
gave them names,
such as "Frank" and
"Lulu" and "Granny."
They called the one-legged
seagull "Sandy." Sometimes, they
would all gather around Ollie to watch
him do acrobatic stunts. Ollie could do a headstand
and a handstand. He could even walk on his hands!

One afternoon, the children were playing "catch-the-morsels" with the one-legged seagull. They would throw pieces of bread into the air, and Sandy would catch them.

After catching a particularly large morsel, Sandy flew high above the shed and disappeared. The one-legged seagull didn't come back that day . . . or the next day . . . or the day after that. Day after day, Sophie and her friends sat and waited.

"Where is Sandy?" they wondered sadly.

One day while they were waiting for Sandy, a storm came up, so the children all went into Sophie's house. They watched from a window as rain splashed against the shed and onto the trash cans. Thunder boomed, lightning flashed, and the ground was soon soggy.

"Maybe Sandy got sick," said Hannah, "or hurt."

"Maybe Sandy is lying somewhere in a puddle," said Pete, "or Carl's cat caught it."

Sophie was already thinking the same things. Poor, poor Sandy.

After the thunderstorm, the children ran outside to the shed and called Sandy's name. Other seagulls were hopping around, drying their wings, but the one-legged seagull was not among them.

Sophie's father was mending his fishing nets nearby.

"Why don't you play hide-and-seek?" he asked.

But the children didn't feel like playing.

The next day, Sophie and Ollie went to the seashore. High above the water, seagulls drifted in the wind, playing catch and swooping down over the sea. Sophie looked at them through her telescope, hoping to see Sandy.

"Let me see," Ollie begged. Sophie hesitated, then gave the telescope to Ollie. It was the very first time she had let anyone else use her telescope.

Ollie saw the waves and the rocks and the boats.

"There!" he cried suddenly. "There's Sandy!"

Sophie grabbed the telescope. Sure enough! She saw the one-legged seagull, doing acrobatic stunts in the air.

All afternoon, Sophie and
Ollie watched Sandy and the
other seagulls swoop and dive.

"What fun!" said Sophie,
as she and Ollie
took turns looking
through the telescope.

And they laughed together
with delight.